Kofi

and

His

By Maya Angelou

**Photographs by
Margaret
Courtney-Clarke**

Magic

**Designed by
Alexander Isley Design**

**Clarkson Potter / Publishers
New York**

Published by Clarkson N. Potter/Publishers,
201 East 50th Street, New York, New York 10022.
Member of the Crown Publishing Group.
Random House, Inc. New York, Toronto, London,
Sydney, Auckland

http://www.randomhouse.com/

CLARKSON N. POTTER, POTTER, and colophon
are trademarks of Clarkson N. Potter, Inc.
Printed in China

Library of Congress Cataloging-in-Publication Data
Angelou, Maya.
Kofi and his magic/by Maya Angelou; photographs
by Margaret Courtney-Clarke. —1st ed.
p. cm.
Summary: A young Ashanti boy describes some of
the wonders of his life in and around the West
African village of Bonwire.
1. Children, Ashanti—Social life and customs—
Juvenile literature. 2. Kente cloth—Ghana—
Bonwire—Juvenile literature. 3. Bonwire (Ghana)—
Social life and customs—Juvenile literature.
[1. Ashanti (African people) 2. Ghana—Social life
and customs.] I. Courtney-Clarke, Margaret,
1949- ill. II. Title.
DT507.A54 1996   96-29210
966.7'004963385—dc20   CIP
AC

ISBN 0-517-70453-6 (trade edition)
ISBN 0-517-70796-9 (GLB edition)
10 9 8 7 6 5 4 3 2 1
First Edition

I dedicate my work in this
book to my late sister
Efua Sutherland and all
the children of Ghana who
were her children too.
—M.A.

For Emmanuel, Erik,
and the twins
Beatrice No. 1 and
Beatrice No. 2.
—M.C.-C.

Hi.

My name is Kofi, and I am a magician.

No, wait now...

My name is Kofi,

I live in West Africa,

the most beautiful

place in the whole

world, and I am

seven years old.

And I am a magician.

I live near the Ashanti golden stool, which everyone knows is pure magic.

The stool is made of
gold and only the
Ashanti king can sit
on it. When he does,
he becomes so powerful
that everyone must
obey his commands.

That's magic.

You may think I'm kidding when I say I'm a magician,

but when I finish my story I'm sure you will believe me.

Okay, first I am, as I
said, Kofi, which means
I am a boy born on
Friday, and I am
a weaver. I weave
Kente cloth, the most
beautiful and richest
cloth in the world.

You may think I am not old enough to be a weaver,

but I began learning years ago when I was young.

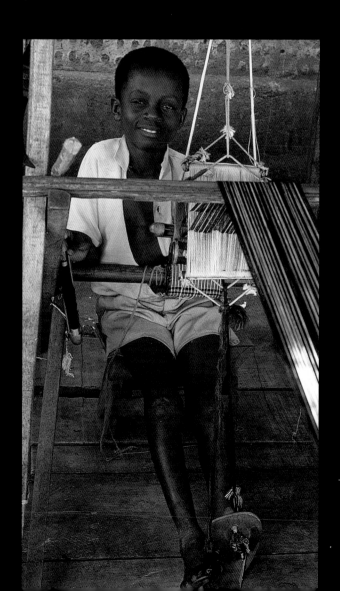

I joined a class of boys learning to weave. The teacher tied threads to our toes and then we would move our feet a little like riding a bicycle. Just a little.

It was hard, but we had fun wiggling our toes, and I could make the threads behave.

But that's not why I am a magician.

My town is called Bonwire, and it is the most famous town in all the

world for Kente weaving.

I don't tell everyone, but I can do a magic thing and make

what I want to come true, come true.

For example...I know Bonwire is the best town in the world, but sometimes I want to go to other places...like the north where people live in houses different from ours, and wear different clothes, and speak differently, and eat different foods.

I also like to hear the names of their towns, Tamale, Sunyani, and Bolgatanga.

So,

I sit down,
Close my eyes,
And open my
mind,

and I am on a bus, waving good-bye

GHANA PE

to my friends in Bonwire.

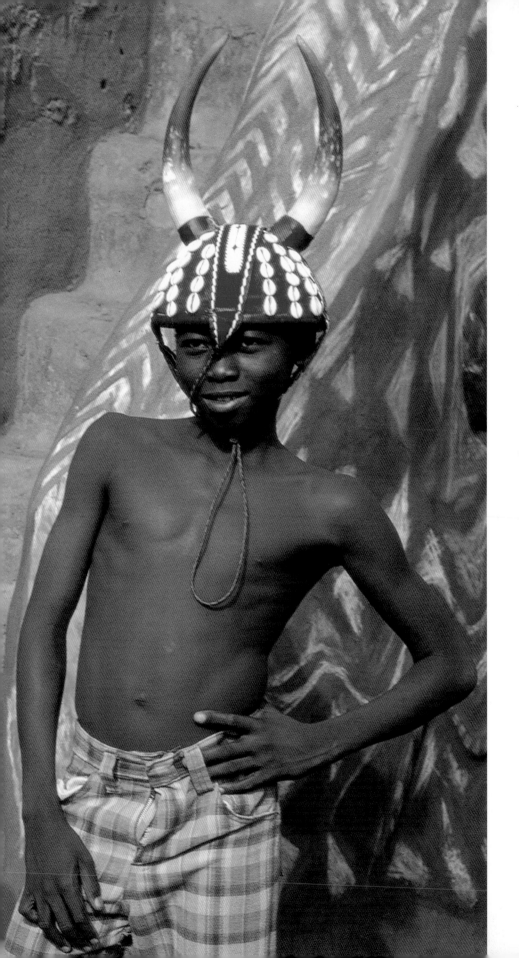

Then, suddenly, I am in the north.

Up here, no one weaves Kente, but they make other cloth. The boys wear hats made with horns and cowrie shells. If I wore a hat like that, I would feel very brave.

When I first see the northern women painting their houses, I laugh because Ashanti women don't do that.

But, then I see how beautiful the houses are when they are finished, and I think it would be magical to live in a painted house.

The northern people like me.

They give me a smock like a big shirt to wear and let me

When I am ready
to go home,

stand with their wise old men.

I sit down,
Close my eyes,
Open my mind,

And I'm back in Bonwire going to school.

We carry our desks to write on

and stools to sit

on because most

of the time classes are outside.

During the rainy

season, we go

inside a building

to study.

Sometimes I get

bored and have

to use my magic.

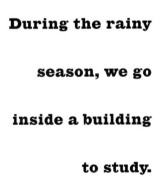

I sit down,
Close my eyes,
Open my mind,

And I am at a festival called a **Durbar.** Every year at harvest time, **the people celebrate.** Powerful chiefs, some of whom are women priests, and wise men **put on their richest Kente and gold** and they are carried through the streets on palanquins **under beautiful umbrellas.**

Dancers and drummers
fill the roads.
With singers singing,
children shouting,
and the *thump, thump*
of the drums,

the noise is wonderful.

There is delicious food to eat everywhere.

I love the Durbar, but I do get tired, so

**I sit down,
Close my eyes,
Open my mind,**

and I am
back home
in Bonwire
with my friend
Kojo who
doesn't laugh
very much.

I decide to share my magic with Kojo.

I tell him we should go to the sea, and I say

Sit down,
Close your eyes,
Open your mind,

And...

I have to repeat myself many times, but at last we both

Sit down,
Close our eyes,
Open our minds,

and then we are at a lake so   wide and blue that we become afraid.

But someone tells us that what we are looking at is not a lake, but the **Atlantic Ocean.**

It has a wonderful
smell and a wonderful
roar like a soft roll of
thunder in the raining
season, and the water
tastes salty.... After a
while, Kojo wants to
go home, so we

Sit down,
Close our eyes,
Open our minds,

And we are back in Bonwire.

I told you at first that I was a magician. Well, I have been thinking in my language, Ashanti, and you have been hearing me in English. So, I think you must be a magician too.

If you ever want to meet me, just

Sit down,
Close your eyes,
Open your mind,

and think about a friend you have in West Africa named Kofi.